Princess Madison
and the Paisley Puppy

KAREN SCALF LINAMEN

ILLUSTRATED BY PHYLLIS HORNUNG

Revell

Grand Rapids, Michigan

Text © 2007 by Karen Scalf Linamen
Illustrations © 2007 by Phyllis Hornung

Published by Fleming H. Revell
a division of Baker Publishing Group
P.O. Box 6287, Grand Rapids, MI 49516-6287
www.revellbooks.com

Printed in the United States of America

Library of Congress Cataloging-in-Publication Data is on file at the Library of Congress, Washington DC.

ISBN 10: 0-8007-1841-0
ISBN 978-0-8007-1841-1

For our Princess Gabriella and the Royal Trio of Isaac,

Hunter, and Connor, beloved sons of the King

Princess Madison loved to visit the royal kennel where her father's hunting dogs lived. Madison loved *all* the happy, eager dogs with their sloppy, eager mouths, but her heart belonged to one silky yellow puppy named Zorobelle.

madison wanted a puppy of her own more than anything else in the whole wide world.

You're probably thinking, *Madison is a princess! Princesses get whatever they want, don't they?*

But they don't, not really, not even prissy pretend princesses in fairy tales, and Madison is very much a real-girl princess, the kind with dirt under her nails and holes in her jeans and freckles on her face. She also has a mom and dad who love her too much to give her everything she wants. They don't want Madison to become a whiney, pouty, spoiled princess, which is the very worst kind of princess of all.

Zorobelle washed Madison's face with kisses. Madison laughed. "I couldn't have said it better myself, Zorobelle. Today is the perfect day to ask Mother if you can come live in the castle with me."

madison found her mother in the garage, welding a statue out of hubcaps.

Madison blurted, "Mom, I would like a puppy of my own more than anything else in the whole wide world, and I love Zorobelle more than any other dog in the universe. I'll feed her and walk her and give her all of her baths. Please can she live with us in the castle? Pleasepleaseplease?"

Madison's mother pinched her chin. "I don't think you know how much work puppies can be. But I will make a deal with you. If you help Mr. Herringbone feed the dogs and clean the royal kennel for two weeks, I will think about letting Zorobelle come live with us in the castle."

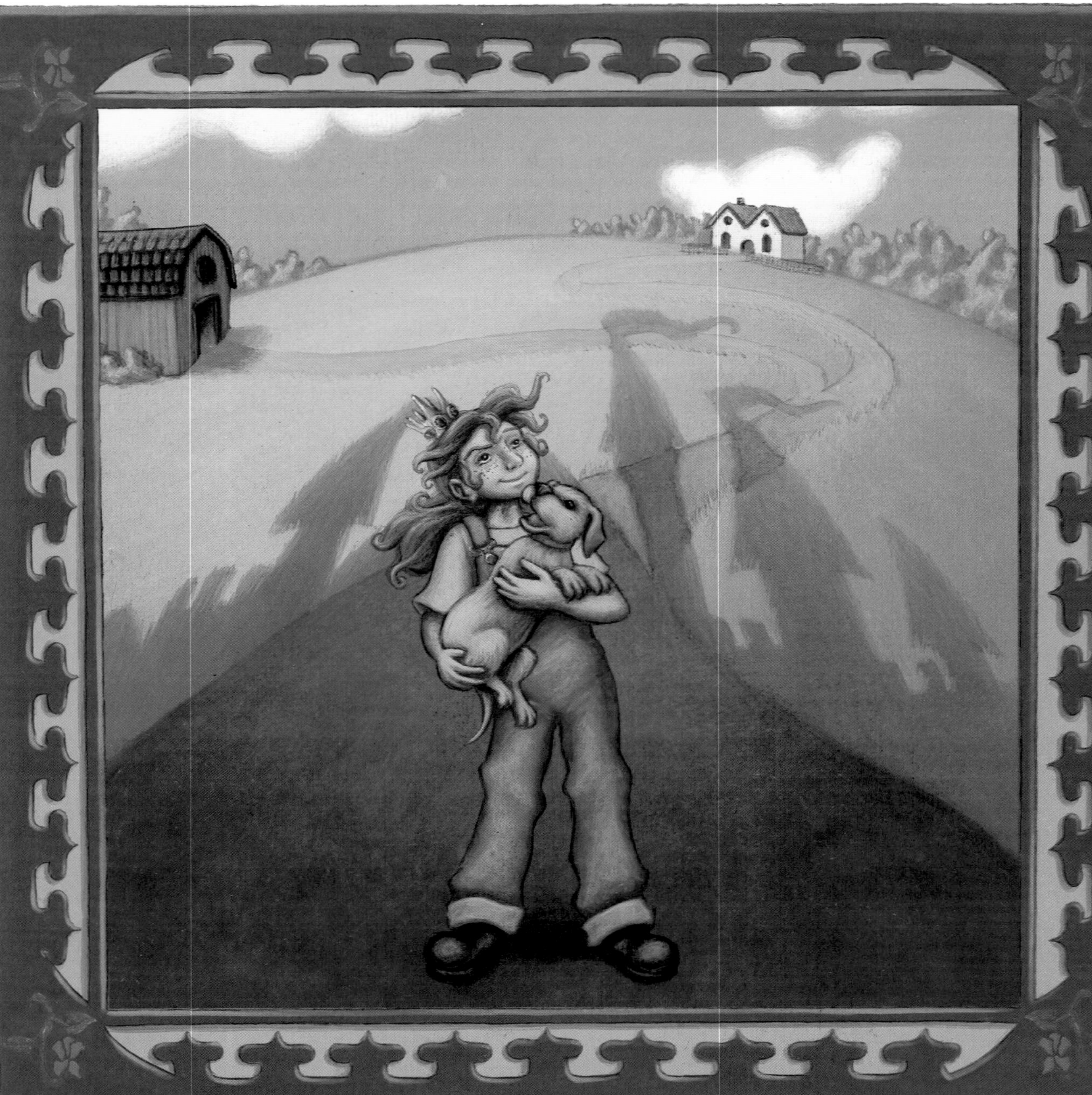

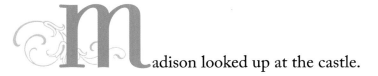adison looked up at the castle.

"That's a very big castle. You're a very little dog. I don't think anyone would even know if you came to live with me.

"Why should I have to help Mr. Herringbone clean the kennel? I already know how much trouble you'll be, and you'll be no trouble at all, Zorobelle! No trouble at all!"

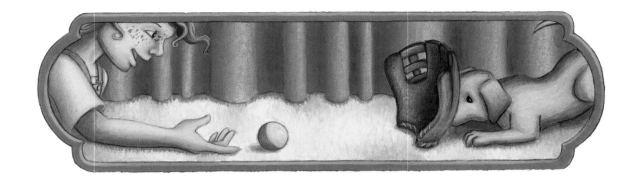

Zorobelle and Madison played catch.

They played with makeup and curlers.

Madison taught Zorobelle to roll over and sit. Zorobelle even got to wear Madison's princess tiara.

After a while Madison looked at her puppy and wondered, *Could she be hungry? I don't have any dog food—not a single bit.*

"I'll be right back," Madison promised.

Zorobelle wagged her tail.

madison sneaked down the stairs and into the kitchen. She was putting something in her pocket when Cook walked into the room.

"What are you doing?" demanded Cook.

"Um, I'm borrowing bologna," explained Madison.

"Why in the Wide World of Sports are you borrowing bologna?" said Cook.

"I forgot to eat breakfast," Madison lied.

"I thought you hated bologna," said Cook.

Madison lied again. "I only hate bologna when it's in a *sandwich*. That's why I'm putting it in my *pocket* instead."

"Aah," said Cook.

Madison hurried out of the kitchen. Okay, so maybe Zorobelle was a *little* bit of trouble after all.

Zorobelle ate up all the bologna.

Madison poured water into a Frisbee, and Zorobelle lapped that up too.

They played hide-and-seek, fetch, chase, and checkers. They painted in Madison's coloring book with watercolors. Then Zorobelle stretched out on Madison's bedspread and fell into a deep puppy sleep.

Madison looked at the clock. It was almost time for lunch. Then she looked at Zorobelle, a bright yellow patch on the purple paisley bedspread. What if someone came into Madison's room while she was gone? How could Madison hide Zorobelle so no one would find her?

Madison knew exactly what to do.

In the kitchen, Madison sat at the table next to her sister, Evangeline. (Evangeline is eleven and thinks she's perfect.)

Madison said, "You stink."

Evangeline pointed her nose in the air. "I'm wearing strawberry-kiwi perfume. Some people think it smells good."

Madison said, "Fruit bats aren't people."

"You two stop bickering," said Cook. She put two plates on the table. On Evangeline's plate there was a bologna sandwich and chips. On Madison's plate there were three pieces of bologna and chips.

Madison wrinkled her nose. "I hate bologna."

"You hate bologna *sandwiches*," Cook reminded Madison. "You like bologna by itself, remember?"

Madison couldn't wait for lunch to end. She wished she hadn't told a lie. She wished she could turn into some kind of animal that liked bologna. Like a cat. Or a silky yellow puppy. Maybe even a fruit bat.

After lunch, Madison ran up the stairs, opened her bedroom door, and called, "Zorobelle, I'm home!"

Ugh! Her room smelled awful. Worse than bologna. Worse than perfume! What was it? What was that smell?

Madison cleaned up Zorobelle's mess. She sighed. "I thought having a puppy would be no trouble. I forgot you need food. I forgot you need a place to go potty."

Zorobelle whimpered and scratched at the bedroom door.

Madison added, "And I forgot you need to play outside."

Tucking Zorobelle in her shirt, Madison tiptoed through the hallway, down the stairs, and past the kitchen.

She was sneaking past her father's study when suddenly the back door of the castle flew open. Laughter and voices got louder and louder.

Madison needed somewhere to hide. She knew just the place!

madison ran into her father's study. She opened the creaky lid of the wood bin next to the fireplace and crawled inside.

It was dark and scary and spidery. Zorobelle whimpered. Madison whispered, "Don't worry, Zorobelle. We'll hide here until everyone goes to the kitchen to make dinner. Then we'll sneak outside and play."

Just then Madison's father said, "I have a great idea! Let's have an inside picnic! We'll invite Cook and Sir Ohmygoodness to join us. We'll put a blanket on the floor in my study. We'll have Eggo waffles and Dr Pepper for dinner."

Madison's mother clapped her hands together. "Madison will be *so* happy. She *loves* Dr Pepper and waffles! By the way, where *is* Madison?"

Evangeline said, "Madison ate bologna for lunch, then ran to her room. She probably has a stomachache. I'm sure she'll come down when she's hungry."

Thanks to Evangeline, no one would go looking for Madison. If only the wood bin were just a little more comfortable.

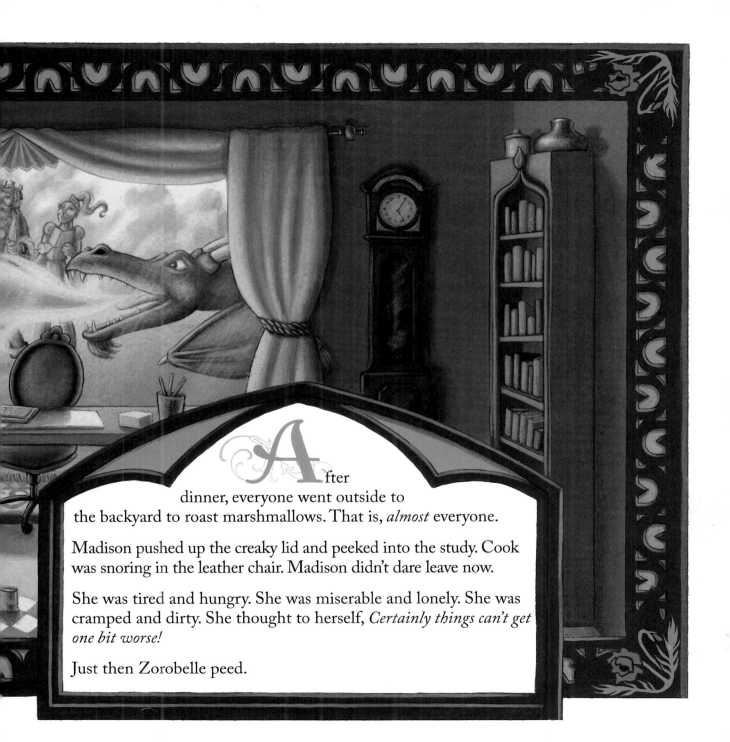

After dinner, everyone went outside to the backyard to roast marshmallows. That is, *almost* everyone.

Madison pushed up the creaky lid and peeked into the study. Cook was snoring in the leather chair. Madison didn't dare leave now.

She was tired and hungry. She was miserable and lonely. She was cramped and dirty. She thought to herself, *Certainly things can't get one bit worse!*

Just then Zorobelle peed.

madison must have fallen asleep, because the next thing she knew, she heard voices.

"Good night, Evangeline," said the queen.

"Good night, Mom."

"Good night, sweetheart," said the king.

"Good night, Dad."

After a while Madison heard typing and knew her mother had logged on to the computer to see how her stocks were doing.

She smelled her father's cigar and knew he was sitting in the leather chair, reading the newspaper.

Madison's feet seemed to be missing. She felt around and touched a sneaker with her hand. Oh, there they were. She was awake, but her legs were still asleep. She had been in the wood bin too long.

Pushing the creaky lid wide open, she crawled into the light. She tried to stand, but her sleeping legs began to tingle so bad that she sat right back down on the floor and started to cry.

uddenly her father was beside her. He said, "Don't move, Madison. Your legs will feel better in a minute."

Zorobelle scampered free, and Madison leaned into her father's embrace. "I got a puppy," she blurted.

Her father said, "I know."

She said, "I lied about my puppy to Cook."

"I know."

She said, "I tried to disguise my puppy to look like my bedspread. And then I took my puppy and hid, but it was dark and cramped and lonely—and then she peed on me!"

The king smiled. "Oh, I know!"

"I thought having a secret puppy would be fun," Madison said. "But it didn't turn out like I thought it would."

He nodded. "Secrets are like that."

"Am I in trouble?" Madison asked.

"What do you think?" her father asked back.

"I think I'd rather be in trouble with you than spend one more minute hiding in that nasty old wood bin!" Then Madison asked, "Daddy, do you still love me?"

The king laughed, a laugh as big as the sky and deep as the ocean.

"Daughter, I love you when you're in trouble and I love you when you're not. I love you when you make good choices or bad, when you are grumpy or when you are sad. When you're right here safe in my arms—or even when you choose to hide—you belong to me and I love you still."

Madison smiled. "Does that mean I get to keep Zorobelle?"

"I confessed all my sins to you and stopped trying to hide them
. . . and you forgave me!"
Psalm 32:5